Fantastic Fairy Tales

CINDERELLA

An imprint of Om Books International

There once lived a girl whose name was Ella. When her dear mother died, everything changed in Ella's life. For, her father brought home a new wife, who only cared for her own two proud, ill-mannered daughters.

Now, these two daughters made their poor little stepsister do all the work.

When everything was done, she would meekly creep near the kitchen fire and rest among the cinders.

“Sitting among the cinders as usual!” her stepmother would cry. “You ought to be called Cinder-Ella instead of Ella.”

Cinderella and her family lived in the kingdom of a kind and generous king, who loved his son dearly.

The prince was now twenty-one years old, and to celebrate his birthday, a splendid ball was to be held at the royal palace.

Invitations were sent out far and near, and much was the delight of Cinderella's stepsisters when they too received an invitation. The invitation was meant for all the young maidens of the household, but no one bothered to ask Cinderella to the royal ball. She was just a servant girl for them!

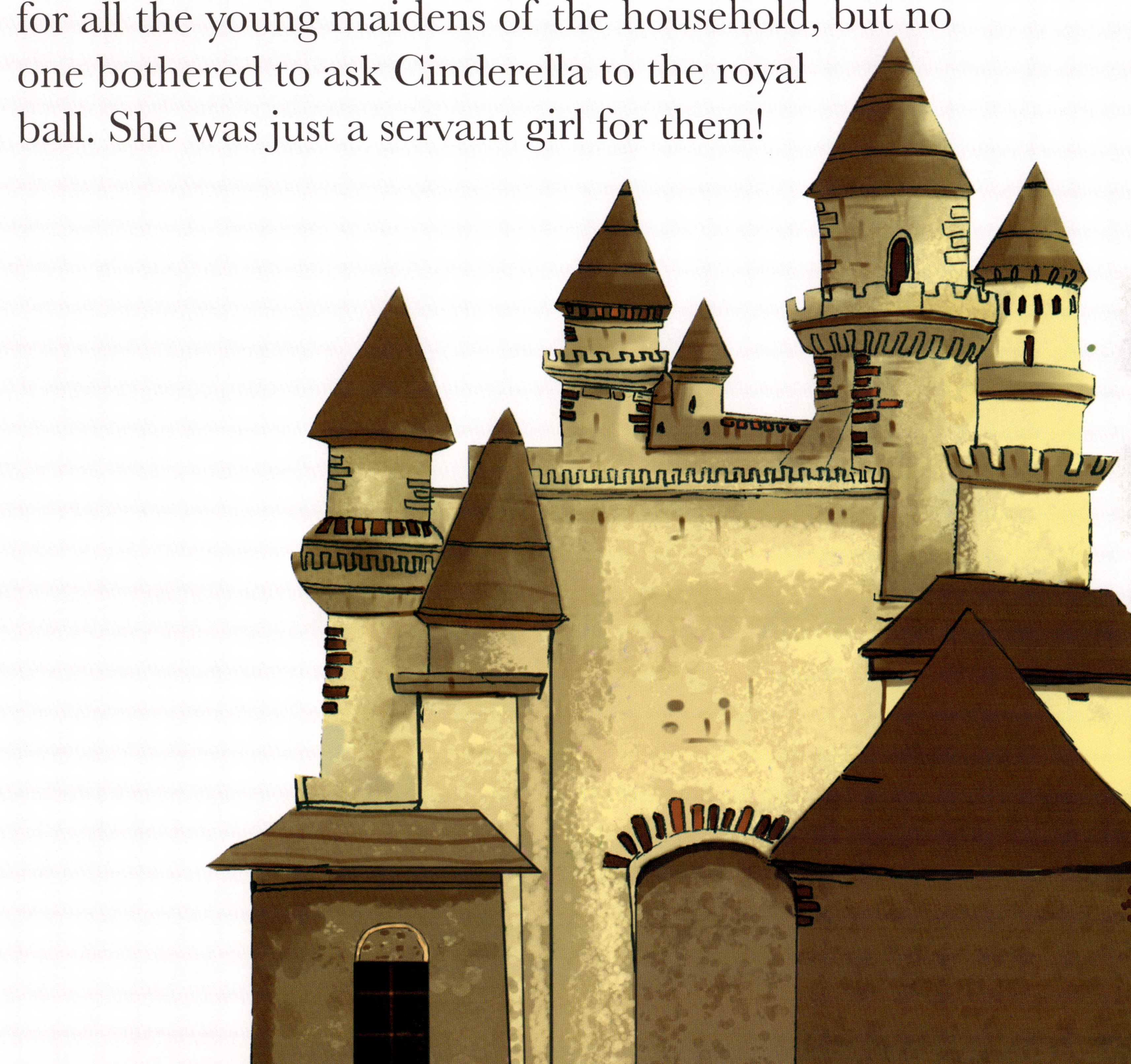

Cinderella was sad but said nothing. She finished her chores and cried herself to sleep that night.

Cinderella sobbed as if her heart would break.

There by the window, through which the new moon could be seen, stood a little old lady watching her. She was dressed in a beautiful long gown and a hat that added to her majesty, and in her hand she held a magic wand.

She said, “Dear little sweet Cinderella! What makes you cry? Your Fairy Godmother is here now. Tell me, what do you want?”

“Oh, Godmother dear,” cried Cinderella, her eyes shining with tears. “I really want to go to the royal ball. Can you help me?”

"Of course, my dear!" said the fairy. "You will go by all means. You will go like a princess in a splendid coach. It's time for a little swish and swoosh of my magic wand."

The Fairy Godmother waved her magic wand. In an instant, there appeared a golden coach driven by six majestic ponies, a dandy old coachman and two footmen in smart red liveries.

She waved her magic wand once more, and the old ragged frock which Cinderella wore turned into the most beautiful robe of shining silk, which looked as if it had been woven from moonbeams and spangled with silver stars.

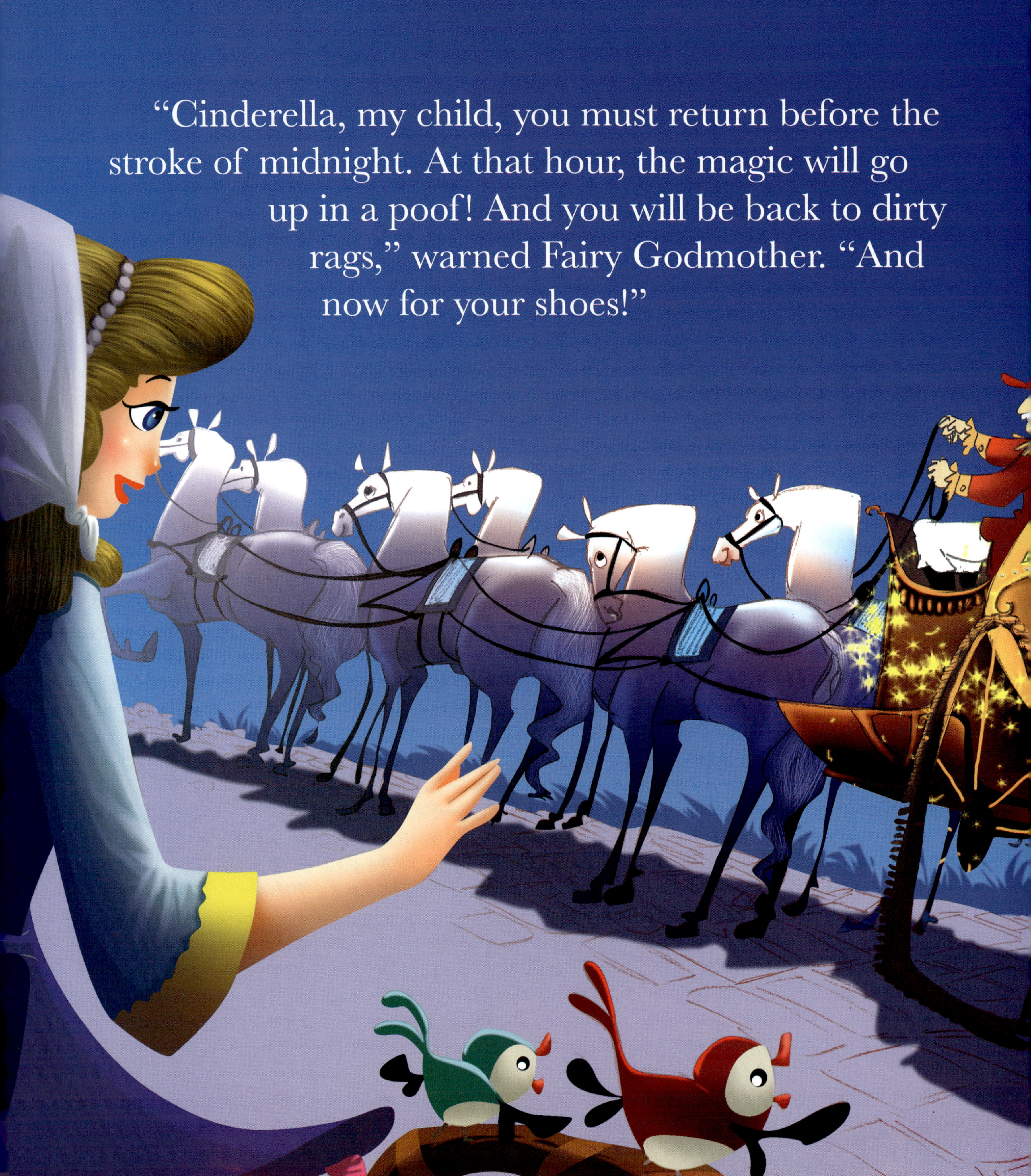

"Cinderella, my child, you must return before the stroke of midnight. At that hour, the magic will go up in a poof! And you will be back to dirty rags," warned Fairy Godmother. "And now for your shoes!"

The Fairy Godmother took out of her pocket the most exquisite little pair of glass slippers, which fitted Cinderella as if they had been made for her.

Cinderella stepped into the golden coach and the six beautiful and swift ponies went off like the wind.

The dancing had just begun at the palace. All the fair ladies were wondering who would be asked to open the ball with the prince, when a beautiful stranger entered the ballroom. The prince held his breath; he had never seen anyone so beautiful.

Everyone turned to look at her, and Cinderella's proud sisters whispered to each other, "What a lovely dress! She must be a princess."

All night long, the prince danced with no one but the beautiful stranger. Cinderella was so happy that she forgot to look at the clock.

For Cinderella and the prince, it was love at first sight. Lost in the loving gaze of the prince, Cinderella heard the loud gong of the clock strike twelve!

"Oh, I almost forgot!" she cried, as she remembered her Godmother's warning.

She hurriedly rushed out of the palace. But in her haste, she tripped and one of her glass slippers came off. She could not stop to pick it up for the prince was following close behind, and so she ran on without it. Just as she reached the great door, the last stroke of twelve sounded, and when the prince came running out and asked the guards if anyone had passed that way, they said, "Only a poor girl in rags, Your Highness."

For days, the prince could think of nothing else but the beautiful lady he had seen at the ball. She came like a whiff of fresh air and vanished as quickly. The prince lost all interest in life. Lost and forlorn, he would not eat, drink or sleep properly.

The king could hardly bear the plight of his dear son and when he asked his son the reason for his gloom, the prince spoke out his heart.

The prince said, “Dear Father, I cannot live without the beautiful lady I met at the ball. I have decided to marry her, but I know nothing of her except that this glass slipper belongs to her.”

Next day, the king sent heralds throughout the kingdom with a royal proclamation.

"To each and every subject of our kingdom, let it be known that last night a glass slipper was found in the royal palace, and whomsoever it shall fit, she alone shall be the prince's bride."

When the herald arrived at the house where Cinderella lived, the proud sisters were so excited that their hands trembled. The two sisters tried their best to fit into the glass slipper, but their feet were just too large!

Meanwhile Cinderella had crept quietly into the room, and as the herald picked up the glass slipper, she asked in a low voice, "Please, may I try it on?"

"Ha! You are just a servant girl, the prince will never marry you!" cried the sisters.

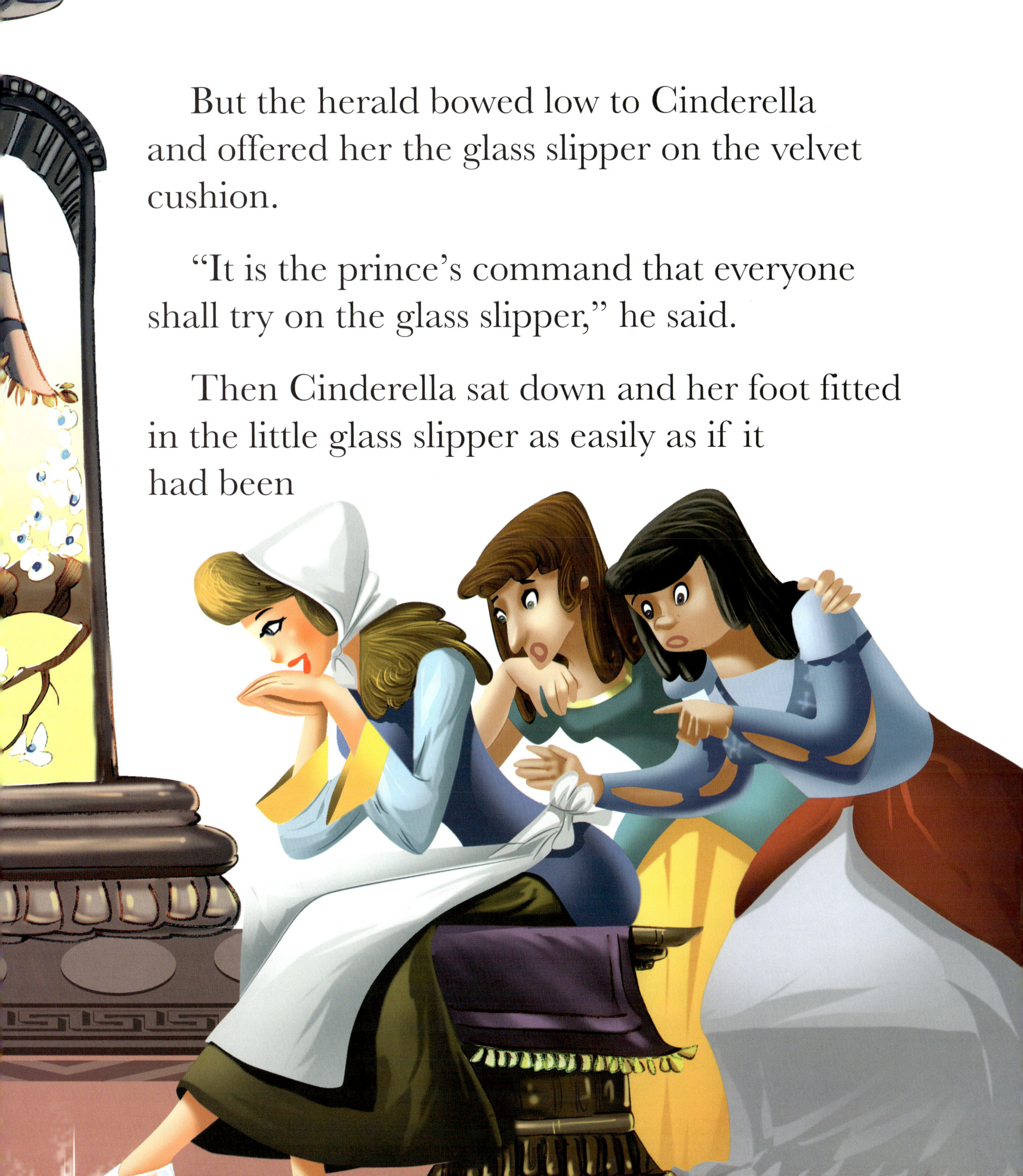

But the herald bowed low to Cinderella and offered her the glass slipper on the velvet cushion.

"It is the prince's command that everyone shall try on the glass slipper," he said.

Then Cinderella sat down and her foot fitted in the little glass slipper as easily as if it had been made for her. While everyone stared in surprise, she took out from her pocket the other slipper which matched it.

"It certainly fits her," smiled the herald.

"Take it off at once!" screamed the two sisters.

But before they could snatch away the slipper, the Fairy Godmother stood in front of Cinderella and waved her magic wand.

And in an instant, the old ragged dress vanished, and there stood the beautiful lady of the ball, in her dress of woven moonbeams spangled with silver stars.

The prince did not wait to ask if the glass slipper had fit her, for he knew his beautiful lady at once, and the wedding bells were rung that very day.

And so, Cinderella married the prince and lived happily ever after.